For Finn   For James
G.McC.   P.H.

VIKING

Published by the Penguin Group
Penguin Putnam Books for Young Readers, 345 Hudson Street, New York, New York 10014, USA
Penguin Books Ltd, 80 Strand, London WC2R 0RL, England
Penguin Books Australia Ltd, Ringwood, Victoria, Australia
Penguin Books Canada Ltd, 10 Alcorn Avenue, Toronto, Ontario, Canada M4V 3B2
Penguin Books (NZ) Ltd, 182-190 Wairau Road, Auckland 10, New Zealand

Penguin Books Ltd, Registered Offices: 80 Strand, London WC2R 0RL, England

First published in Great Britain in Puffin Books, 2002
First published in the United States of America by Viking, a division of Penguin Putnam Books for Young Readers, 2002

1 3 5 7 9 10 8 6 4 2

Text copyright © Geraldine McCaughrean, 2002
Illustrations copyright © Paul Howard, 2002
All rights reserved.
Library of Congress Cataloging-in-Publication Data is available
ISBN 0–670–03588–2

Printed in China
Set in Poliphilus MT

ONE BRIGHT PENNY

GERALDINE MCCAUGHREAN

PAUL HOWARD

VIKING

It was pocket-money day. Every Friday, Bill and Bob and Penny were each given one bright penny.

Every Friday, they had to listen to their pa telling them, "I remember when a penny was worth something, and I could buy a new pair of boots for only five pennies. Those were the good old days!"

He had said it many times.

"In those days I could have filled that there old barn with winter feed for a penny. Children these days don't know the value of money no more."

Usually, Bill, Bob, and Penny bent their heads over their porridge and kept silent. But today Bill said, "I bet I could fill the barn for one penny!"

For the first time that year, the old man laughed. "If one of you can fill the barn for a penny, I'll give you the farm and go live in the chicken coop, and that's a promise!"

Old Pa was still laughing as he gave out the pocket money:

a penny to Bill,   a penny to Bob,   and one to Penny.

"Try it!" he snickered. "Do! In fact, if you can't, I won't pay you no more pocket money, you hear?"

Out he went to pick greenfly off the roses, and the children were left sitting openmouthed.

"Now look what you've done!" said Bob.

"Don't fret," said Bill. "I'll think of something."

Bill walked down the road to the turkey farm next door.

The ground inside the fence was downy with bright feathers.

In went Bill and said to the owner, "How many feathers will you sell me for one penny?"

"Take all you like. No charge," said the turkey farmer. "But for a penny you can rent the bags to carry them home in."

So all day, Bill went to and fro, to and fro, filling sacks with feathers, cramming them in. The turkeys came gobbling after him, angry and terrifying; the feathers made him sneeze. He worked till every last sack was full.

Every cartload he brought home was a bulging mountain of feathery sacks.

Next day, he took the sacks into the old barn and emptied them out again.

A snow of feathers.

A blizzard of feathers.

Whiteout.

Bill sneezed and coughed, pushed and patted and plumped.

That evening, Pa had just got home from picking sheep's wool off the fences when Bill burst in.

"Mercy me, it's an ostrich!" cried Penny.

"It's the Abominable Snowman!" cried Bob.

"Gosh sakes, boy," said Pa, "what you been doing? Turkey wrestling?"

"I've been filling the barn," said Bill through a mouthful of feathers. "Come and see."

So the family trooped out to the barn, and Pa opened the big barn doors.

A wall of feathers greeted him. "Bet it ain't full right up to the rafters," he said, remembering his promise.

"Right up to the roof ridge. Take a look," replied Bill. So they all climbed up a ladder, to check that the barn was full.

But just as he opened the hayloft doors, a feather tickled Bill's nose and he sneezed a gigantic sneeze.

A flurry of feathers plumed out of the barn and floated slowly down, leaving a little hole in the tightly packed whiteness.

"Told you!" crowed Pa. "Nice try, sonny, but the barn ain't full!" And for the second time that year, he laughed, while the barn leaked feathers like a molting duck.

Now it was Bob's turn. While turkey feathers drifted by outside like snow, Bob considered how he might fill the barn with just one penny.

Then he went out to the chandler's store and bought himself a ball of string and a big block of wax.

All day he worked in his room. Bill and Penny could hear the snip of scissors and the drip-drip of liquid. When they peeped through the keyhole, the room seemed to be hung with icicles, like the cave of a hibernating bear.

Next evening, the room was empty.

Pa had spent all day throwing stones at the crows in the cornfield. He was tired and grumpy and he wanted his supper.

But Bob danced him out of the house and across the yard to the barn, saying, "I filled it! I filled it, Pa! See for yourself!"

Out through every gap and knothole, where the tiles were missing and under the barn door, flowed a flicker of gold. Bob lifted the latch and opened the door, and for a moment all four gaped and gasped at what they saw.

A thousand candles had filled the barn with light.

Then the old man broke into a jigging dance and threw his hat in the air. "T'aint full! T'aint full! Looky there!"

It had taken a long time to light all the candles. The last ones alight were burning merrily. But the very first one had burned all the way down and gone out, leaving nothing but a puddle of melted wax. Darkness the shape of a cobweb lodged in that one lightless corner.

Then a draft from the open door blew out every rank and row of candles and left the four staring into darkness.

For the third time that year, the old man laughed out loud. "Nice try, sonny, but the farm's still mine. Tee hee hee!"

That left Penny.

If she could not fill the barn with just one penny, there would be no more pocket money for any of them.

Penny did not waste time thinking. She took her pocket money to town.

With only one penny a week there had always been things that needed buying—birthday presents or new socks, school books, Christmas decorations or candy for her brothers.

But now she went to the old junk shop on the corner and picked out what she had wanted for herself, all life long.

"This for you, Penny?" asked the shopkeeper lifting it down.

"Yep. Just for me."

She took it home and cleaned it. She mended and glued it.

She was busy night and morning, come-day, go-day, week in and week out.

On pocket-money days there were no bright pennies for anyone, only a mean, dry old chuckle from Pa. Penny did not mind; she was busy in her room, fixing and waxing.

Then one evening, Pa came home from collecting old horseshoe nails. He found the yard full of trucks and people and dogs. All the neighbors had come round.

"We heard there was a party," they said, "so we came right over."

Pa could hear music. He looked in the house, but no one was there. As he crossed the yard, the music got louder. There was singing too.

He opened up the barn, and there sat Penny, on a bale of hay, a battered old banjo on her knees, playing hell-for-leather, while the neighbors danced and sang and whooped.

For the fourth time that year the old man laughed. "You foolish great lummocking girl! I thought you were brighter than your brothers, but here you are a bigger fool than either. Did you think you could fill the barn with neighbors?"

"Don't talk foolish, Pa!" said Penny still plink-plank-plunking at her shiny banjo. "But take a listen and tell me: haven't I filled the barn with music?"

Well, Pa climbed up the ladder to the hayloft. He went round the back and back around to the front. He climbed up on the roof ridge. He opened the door to let in a draft and he sneezed till his hat fell off…but there was no denying it. Penny had filled the old barn right up to the roof. There wasn't a corner or a cranny that wasn't full of music.

Pa wasn't laughing anymore. "Reckon the farm's yours," he said, remembering his promise. "Always knew you were a bright girl, Penny. I'll just go and make my bed up in the chicken coop."

"Don't be silly, Pa! I want to join a band! Give the farm to Bob and Bill. It's time you quit working and put your feet up: I'll supply the music."

Then the old man put his head back and laughed—not a dry chuckle or a sneering crow, but a big ringing laugh that filled the old barn right up to the roof beams.